P9-CPZ-322

HOW the Ostrich Got Its LONG Neck

A Tale from the Akamba of Kenya

RETOLD BY VERNA AARDEMA
ILLUSTRATED BY MARCIA BROWN

Scholastic Inc.
NEW YORK

JP

For Maya Ann and Raju Agaskar

— V. A.

For Mae and Sidney Roger

— M. B.

Library of Congress Cataloging-in-Publication Data
Aardema, Verna.
How the ostrich got its long neck / retold by Verna Aardema;
illustrated by Marcia Brown.
p. cm.
Includes bibliographical references (p. 32).
Summary: A tale from the Akamba people of Kenya
that explains why the ostrich has such a long neck.
ISBN 0-590-48367-6
[1. Akamba (African people)—Folklore. 2. Folklore—Kenya.]
I. Brown, Marcia, ill. II. Title.
PZ8.1.A213Ho 1995
398.2'0967620452851—dc20
[E] 94-33642
CIP
AC

12 11 10 9 8 7 6 5 4 3 2 1 5 6 7 8 9/9 0/0

Printed in Singapore 10
First printing, September 1995
This book was illustrated with watercolor and marker on hot press board.
The text type was set in Hiroshige and the display type in Saint Louis Light by WLCR New York, Inc.
Color separations were made by Bright Arts Ltd., Singapore
Printed and bound by Tien Wah Press, Singapore
Production supervision by Angela Biola
Design by Claire B. Counihan

PTB

Long long ago, when the earth was set down and the sky was lifted up, the ostrich had a short neck.

It was most inconvenient, for he had to sit down to catch insects on the ground. And he could not reach berries that were high on the bushes.

Also, when he went to the river, he had to spread his legs wide apart in order to take a drink. But there was a crocodile in that river. And one morning, when the clouds were still pink from the sunrise, Crocodile woke up with a terrible toothache.

Crocodile swam swiftly down the river looking for help, her tears dripping into the water with tiny splashes, *tih*

tih

tih.

Soon Crocodile saw a kudu at the river's edge, lapping, *lop lop lop*. Crocodile called, "Hiye, Kudu, will you take a look at my teeth? I have a terrible toothache. And maybe you could pry out the bad tooth with one of your long twisted horns."

Fish Eagle, who was circling above the river, cried, *"Kwark! Kwark! Don't do it! Don't do it!"*

At the first *kwark,* ducks who were feeding on the shallow side of the river skittered across the water flapping, *kahk-kahk-kahk,* to get airborne. Parrots, hornbills, and finches in the nearby trees flew off, too. And Kudu galloped away, *ka-PU-tu, ka-PU-tu, ka-PU-tu!*

Farther on, Crocodile saw a baboon with a baby on her back, bending over the water's edge.

Crocodile called, "Hiye! Mama Baboon, will you take a look at my teeth? I have a terrible toothache! And maybe you could dig out the bad tooth with your sharp claw."

Fish Eagle, who had followed Crocodile, called, *"Kwark! Kwark! Don't do it! Don't do it!"*

Mama Baboon ran off, *zak-vak-dilak,* with her tail curled over her back, and the baby clinging to her with all his baby strength.

Crocodile swam on, her tears dripping into the water with tiny splashes, *tih*

tih

tih.

Farther on, it happened that the short-necked ostrich was drinking by the edge of the river.

Crocodile called, "Hiye, Ostrich, will you take a look at my teeth? I have a terrible toothache. And I'm sure you could pull out the bad tooth with your strong beak."

Ostrich backed away. He wanted nothing to do with a crocodile.

"Please help me!" begged Crocodile. "I won't hurt you!"

Ostrich moved a little closer. Crocodile paddled to the water's edge and opened her big mouth. A shiver of fear ruffled Ostrich's fluffy coat.

Fish Eagle called down, *"Kwark! Kwark! Don't do it! Don't do it!"*

Ostrich backed farther away. Crocodile cried harder than before. This awakened pity in Ostrich's heart, and he cautiously inched his way back to Crocodile. And again Crocodile opened her mouth.

Ostrich began tapping one tooth after another, *tik tik tik*. "Is this the one that hurts?" he would ask. "Is this the one?"

Each time, Crocodile said,
"Uh-uh, uh-uh, uh-uh."

The big bird's head went deep into Crocodile's mouth. Suddenly, Crocodile remembered that she'd had no breakfast. She clamped her jaws down — *KBAK!* — trapping Ostrich's head.

"Le'-me-ou'," cried Ostrich in a muffled voice. *"Le'-me-ou'!"*

Elephant was bathing nearby. *"EEEEK!"* he squealed. "Crocodile is pulling Ostrich's head off!"

Fish Eagle called from above, “Pull, Ostrich, PULL!”

Ostrich planted his big feet in the sod on the riverbank and pulled. He pulled and pulled and pulled. Crocodile pulled, too, but in the opposite direction.

Ostrich backed up, but Crocodile did not budge. And as Ostrich backed away, his neck stretched longer and *l o n g e r* and *l   o   n   g   e   r!*

Ostrich dragged the big crocodile right out of the water. The hot sun beat down on Crocodile's back and made her tooth hurt worse than before.

When Crocodile finally opened her mouth to say, “Put me back in the water — ” Ostrich escaped! He ran a little way, then he stopped. Something was not right!

The ground seemed much farther away —
but he could reach it easily.

And the berries
high on a nearby bush
were right within
his reach.

What was different? Ostrich wondered. And then he knew. His neck had become long. Very very long. He flapped his wings in delight! Then he strutted off with his head held high, *tuk-pik tuk-pik tuk-pik*.

And since that time, ostriches have stayed in the bush — far from the river. For now, even the youngest ostrich knows better than to trust a hungry crocodile.

A NOTE ABOUT THIS STORY

This tale was told to Bill Gordh, a New York City schoolteacher and storyteller, during his recent travels in Kenya. The Akamba man who gave him the story said his grandmother had often told it to him. He also said that the word "Kenya," which is pronounced KEN-yah, means "the place where there are ostriches."

"How the Ostrich Got Its Long Neck" is a *pourquoi* (por-KWAH) story. *Pourquoi* is a French word that means "why." This type of story usually describes how an animal or person came to have a particular characteristic or how a certain natural phenomenon came to be. This story is similar to "The Elephant's Child," which is in a book called *Just So Stories* by Rudyard Kipling.

Here are some more *pourquoi* stories that you will enjoy:

Aardema, Verna. "Lee Lee Goro," collected in *Misoso: Once Upon a Time Tales from Africa.* Illustrated by Reynold Ruffins. Knopf, 1994.

Aardema, Verna. *Why Mosquitoes Buzz in People's Ears.* Illustrated by Leo and Diane Dillon. Dial Books, 1975.

Bryan, Ashley. *The Cat's Purr.* Atheneum, 1985.

Garland, Sherry. *Why Ducks Sleep on One Leg.* Illustrated by Jean and Mou-sien Tseng. Scholastic Inc., 1993.

McDermott, Gerald. *Raven.* Harcourt Brace, 1993.

Reneaux, J. J., "Why Alligator Hates Dog," collected in *From Sea to Shining Sea,* compiled by Amy L. Cohn. Illustrated by eleven Caldecott Medal and four Caldecott Honor book artists. Scholastic Inc., 1993.

Wolkstein, Diane. "Bye-Bye," collected in *The Magic Orange Tree and Other Haitian Folktales.* Knopf, 1978.

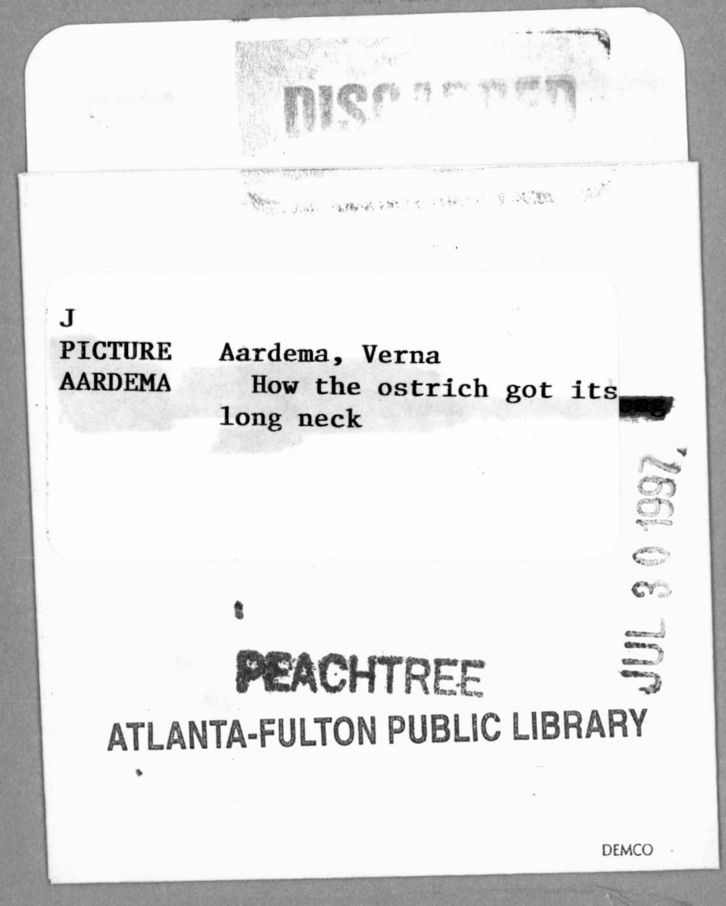
DISCARDED
J
PICTURE
AARDEMA
Aardema, Verna
How the ostrich got its long neck
JUL 30 1997
PEACHTREE
ATLANTA-FULTON PUBLIC LIBRARY
DEMCO